# Awful Arabella

## Bill Gillham

*Illustrated by Margaret Chamberlain*

Methuen Children's Books

Arabella came to stay.

She was awful!

She pulled the cat's tail.

She jumped on the furniture.

She put cornflakes in
her cocoa.

She wouldn't go to bed.

She kept calling out.

But in the night
she was ill.

"I feel awful," said Arabella.

She was sick in the bathroom.

Mummy bathed her face,

and tucked her up in bed.

In the morning
Arabella felt much better,

and she was
*much* better behaved.

She boiled an egg
for Daddy's breakfast.

She washed the cat . . .

and tied a bow on its tail.

She swept the kitchen floor . . .

and blew up the car tyres . . .

and took the baby for a walk.

So why is everyone
looking sad?

Wonderful Arabella
is going away!

## How to pair read

1 Sit the child next to you, so that you can both see the book.

2 Tell the child you are *both* going to read the story *at the same time*. To begin with the child will be hesitant: adjust your speed so that you are reading almost simultaneously, *pointing to the words* as you go.

3 If the child makes a mistake, repeat the correct word but *keep going* so that fluency is maintained.

4 Gradually increase your speed once you and the child are reading together.

5 As the child becomes more confident, lower your voice and, progressively, try dropping out altogether.

6 If the child stumbles or gets stuck, give the correct word and continue 'pair-reading' to support fluency, dropping out again quite quickly.

7 Read the story *right through* once a day but not more than twice, so that it stays fresh.

8 After about 5–8 readings the child will usually be reading the book independently.

*In its original form paired reading was first described by RTT Morgan and E Lyon (1979), in a paper published in the Journal of Child Psychology and Psychiatry.*